Gregory lives in Virginia with his wife, Carithia.

He is a retired executive with AT&T.

He has a love of music and sports.

Dedicated to my wife, my muse, Carithia Williams.

Gregory Williams

LABYRINTH

AUSTIN MACAULEY PUBLISHERS™
LONDON • CAMBRIDGE • NEW YORK • SHARJAH

Ordering Information
Quantity sales: Special discounts are available on quantity purchases by corporations, associations, and others. For details, contact the publisher at the address below.

Publisher's Cataloging-in-Publication data
Williams, Gregory
Labyrinth

ISBN 9798889102229 (Paperback)
ISBN 9798889102243 (ePub e-book)
ISBN 9798889102236 (Audiobook)

Library of Congress Control Number: 2023924466

www.austinmacauley.com/us

First Published 2024
Austin Macauley Publishers LLC
40 Wall Street, 33rd Floor, Suite 3302
New York, NY 10005
USA

mail-usa@austinmacauley.com
+1 (646) 5125767

20240508

I believe there is a wheel of life; a sort of labyrinth or maze-looking thing that has opening and closing gates at various intervals in life. Each of us circles around in this labyrinth at different speeds, and if we are lucky, or prepared, we find an opening that leads to another level. A level with more and perhaps greater life opportunities and understanding. Some people find more openings than others. Some fail to recognize the ones they do find. Regardless, the cycle continues throughout life. Once through a gate, you can never go back.

– Mark Brooks

Chapter One
Mark Brooks

Mark Brooks had just passed through an opening; a life-changing one. After ten years at WQMD as the 2 am to 7 am host of "After Midnight", he felt he had finally found his calling. He had received his law degree and passed the Bar exam. He was now a lawyer, an attorney, a counselor at law. He had done it, and done it the hard way, three nights a week from 6:30 pm to 9:30 pm for four long years. There was a great sense of satisfaction and accomplishment, but now all of that was behind him. Now, there were decisions to be made.

The work at WQMD was especially gratifying. Virtually alone in the studio, Mark was prince of the airwaves. His Soul/R&B repertoire was reminiscent of the music he had heard as a teenager listening to Big John R and the gang on WLAC out of Nashville. The city loved his music, and the light telephone conversations kept everything interesting and moving; the hours felt like minutes.

But something was missing. Since he was a child, he had always felt that he was destined to do something special with his life. A few years back, he thought it may have been politics or even the clergy. Now, in his fifth year of attending SAA, Sex Addicts Anonymous, meetings, it was clear that the skeletons in his closet would have rattled to pieces had he taken either path. Law was different, people didn't seem to mind much if their lawyer had "personal issues", as long as he was able to get them what they wanted.

For Mark, graduating in the middle of his class at a second-tier law school didn't bring offers from any of the local law firms. If he was going to practice full time, he was going to have to hang out a shingle. That meant giving up his DJ "day" job. Lacking both the courage and the financial stability to walk away, he instead spent his free time working wills and insurance cases; cases that didn't require court appearances or long hours of research. It brought in a little extra money and kept him involved in the legal community.

His introduction to SAA had come after years of soul searching in an effort to understand why he did the things he did over and over again. It had been with him since his earliest memories, his obsession with the opposite sex. As a child of five or six, he had been fascinated by the older girls he saw in their short shorts and tank tops in the summer and their tight skirts and sweaters in the winter. As a teen and an adult, his life had revolved around one sexual escapade after another, until his days were often consumed with finding his next conquest. These were mostly one-night stands with women he met at bars, parties, or anywhere else for that matter. They could be married or single; often he was putting his job, his law career, and even his life at risk.

SAA had been more than a blessing. It gave him what he needed to gain control over his behavior and allowed him to be "free from the insanity". The promises of the program were coming true. He had not "acted out" in three years.

It was at an SAA meeting that Mark first saw Howard Goldstein, a balding man with a kind round face and an easy manner. Mark had seen him at several meetings. Howard appeared to be a "Newcomer", one of those people who find their way to an SAA meeting after hitting rock bottom with their spouse, or facing a court appearance join a Twelve Step program in an effort to save their marriage or gain favor with the court system.

It was hard to tell about Howard. He didn't say much at the meetings and didn't hang around long afterwards to talk, so it was a surprise when, after several weeks, Howard asked if he could call and talk.

Having someone trust him enough to want to call was a big deal, especially for Mark, one of the few Black men in the program. His first thought was that Howard needed a sponsor to guide him through recovery and there was something he saw in Mark that made him Howard's choice.

All prepared to give sage advice concerning this cunning, baffling, and powerful addiction, Mark was taken by surprise when Howard called and said he had heard that Mark was a lawyer and wanted some legal advice. How Howard had found out that Mark was a lawyer when everything in SAA was supposed to be anonymous was a question Mark had every intention of asking at the end of the conversation. He decided that until then, he would let Howard talk. Howard said that since Mark was a lawyer and a member of SAA, he felt doubly safe concerning confidentiality and anonymity, and it was safe to talk about the "Problem", as he referred to it.

Chapter Two
The Problem

"Hypothetically speaking, how liable would I be if I knew of a crime and said nothing?"

"You know of a crime hypothetically? Were you hypothetically involved in this crime?"

"I might have been there."

Mark got to the point. "How serious a crime are we talking about?"

"As bad as they get."

"My friend, you need to get a lawyer and go to the police, in that order."

"I can't afford to go public. There are some very influential people involved here."

"Are they influential enough to keep you out of jail?"

"My life could be in danger."

"Look, Howard, you are way out of my league here. I don't see how I can help."

"But if I told you something, as a lawyer you'd have to keep it secret, right?"

"I'm not your lawyer."

"Okay, but the rules of SAA still apply, don't they?"

"Not legally. Why me?"

"Somebody has to know what they did. If something happens to me, somebody they don't know will know who did it, and why. Someone they would never suspect."

Mark listened to Howard's story, wondering if he was being played. Addicts make shit up. The story was too bizarre to be real.

It seems that Howard had been some kind of whiz kid, with a flair for languages and finance. He spoke fluent Arabic, Hindi, Mandarin, Russian, and several other more obscure Eastern and African languages and dialects. He had spent twenty years in the military in counterintelligence and since then traveled the world as a freelance interpreter, off and on working for the U.S. Foreign Service, Fortune 500 companies, and the CIA. His travels and talents brought him into contact with many high-ranking officials and executives in the U.S. and abroad. It seems being an American able to understand, speak, and write in multiple foreign languages was a prized skill in high demand, which endeared him to many an official or corporate executive in both days-long, high-level negotiations and at nights on the town. It was the latter that led to the "Problem".

The reason that Howard was in SAA was his addiction to child pornography; an addiction so crippling it had cost him seven years in Federal prison, and that was with time off for good behavior. He had been out of prison for six years now and working as a waiter at an upscale restaurant downtown. It was the best he could do with a record.

About six months ago, a senior government official named Fred had visited the restaurant and immediately recognized him. After the initial shock of being recognized, something he knew would eventually happen, Howard tried to act as casually as he could. He knew this man from his days in the foreign service. They had spent many a night in the hovels of Asia, Eastern Europe, Africa, and Vietnam with Howard negotiating the preferences and prices for the evening's entertainment—sex with underage girls and boys.

Fred shook Howard's hand like it had just been days since they last saw each other. He was not Fred's waiter, but after dinner, Fred gave Howard his card and told him to call. He took out another card and asked Howard to write down a number that he could reach him on. He immediately copied Howard's number into his Blackberry.

Howard had no intention of calling Fred, there was no need to, with his record there was no chance of any job offer with the government, and it was doubtful, given his present circumstances, that he would be invited to any diplomatic social events. As for Fred taking his number, sharing contact information was simply force of habit for diplomats.

All that changed when Howard received a call inviting him to attend a Texas Hold 'em poker party at Fred's country retreat. It was up north somewhere and Howard wouldn't know anybody there but Fred. Maybe that was all there was to it, a night of poker with the guys.

Howard was picked up by a limousine and chauffeured to an estate just within the city limits. Obviously, Fred had money, more money than any government agency was paying.

Upon arrival, Howard was briefly introduced to five other men. All of them were foreigners from different countries, but all appeared to be accustomed to wealth and privilege. To his surprise, the poker game had a ten-dollar limit.

The game was just an excuse for these men to get together. Due to the ten-dollar limit, the game moved quickly and Howard was doing well. Heavy hors d'oeuvres were plentiful, as was the vintage wine and top shelf liquor. It wasn't until late in the evening, after dinner, that Fred broached the subject of the past.

"We had some grand old times, you and I."

"Long time ago."

"Still, great times. I was telling the guys how your language gifts and negotiation skills made for some very interesting nights."

"All better left in the past."

Howard didn't like the way this conversation was headed. No good could come of it; yet he was trapped out in the middle of nowhere with no way to leave and no easy way to shift the topic without bringing up his addiction, or worse, his incarceration. Fred told Howard to relax. He'd checked him out. He knew all about the conviction and jail time.

'Damn shame.'

Howard was going into great detail, as if he were talking into a recorder. He suddenly paused and Mark could a voice in the background.

"Howard, are you still there?"

"It's my wife. Just a minute dear, I'll be right down. Mark, I've got to go. I'll call you back later."

"Yeah sure, if you want to. Although I'm still not sure what the problem is or how I can help."

"I'll call you later."

Chapter Three
Do the Right Thing

Mark had listened to Howard's story as much out of a sense of telephonic voyeurism than anything else. He did find himself wanting to hear more, especially about the crime Howard had alluded to witnessing.

Howard was not at the next meeting or the two after that. He never called back. Several days later, Mark got a package in his mailbox at the station. As was his custom, he waited until he got home to open his mail. It had no return address and was addressed to Attorney Mark Brooks with an out of state postmark. Inside were newspaper clippings about a young girl sexually assaulted, brutally murdered, and dumped in a wooded area several miles outside the city. It was clear that the body had been moved. Police had no clues and no leads. They believed the girl to be between the ages of twelve and fifteen, probably from out of the country. Mark had seen the articles before in his newspaper but had viewed them as only as a further indication of the rising tide of violent crime in the city.

He stopped reading and turned to the accompanying letter.

I mailed this to you because it's too dangerous for me to talk on the phone at home. I believe my life is in danger because I know too much and I am considered a liability to people who have too much to lose if I talk.

I am partly responsible for this young girl's suffering and death. I personally did not harm her in any way, but I was there, and I did not stop it. I cannot live with this guilt and they know it. It's only a matter of time before they feel it necessary to make sure I don't expose everything and everybody; I've taken some precautions, and one of them is you. They don't know about you. I'm sorry to drag you into this but I am too old to go back to prison and someone has to pay for her death. I know you'll do the right thing.

"I'll do what's right? What the hell does that mean?" Mark said aloud.

The next day, Mark picked up his newspaper. There it was, right there on the Journal's local page: "Silver City man found dead in apparent suicide". The accompanying picture showed a smiling Howard Goldstein from years back. The article did not mention his conviction or prison time. No suicide note was found. Howard had died from asphyxiation in his garage; a cut off garden hose through the window of his car, motor running.

Everyone at the SAA meeting was sure that the addiction had claimed another victim. The group had lost at least four members in the five years since Mark had been attending. Addiction takes its toll. Mark would have thought so too except for his knowledge of Howard's "problem"— the letter and the news clippings.

Howard's death weighed on Mark. He could understand a suicide. Howard had said that he could not go back to prison. He also said he feared for his life from people with the means and motivation to end it.

It wasn't more than a week later that Mark received a letter from an attorney named Ellis J. Dobson. The letter was to notify him that he had been named a beneficiary in the will of Howard Goldstein and the reading was scheduled for that next Tuesday at Howard's former residence. Mark didn't know what to make of this new development. Working as a waiter, it wouldn't appear that Howard had any wealth to leave to anyone.

When he arrived at the house, there were six people in the living room of a moderately priced colonial house near the center of town. He felt extremely out of place, especially since everyone there appeared to be family. No one spoke to him, but he could feel the stares. Finally, Ellis Dobson approached and asked if he was Mark Brooks. That being established, he retreated and conferred with the family.

Mark noticed a striking-looking Asian woman who, judging by her appearance and manner, was Howard's widow. She must have been a trophy wife. She was quite a bit younger than Howard and maybe just a year or two older than Mark. Everyone else, save Attorney Dobson, was clearly a senior citizen. Dobson asked if everyone could be seated and officially began the reading. The four family members turned out to be Howard's siblings, two brothers and two sisters. He would learn later that none of them had seen or spoken to Howard since his conviction and incarceration.

The reading went quickly and predictably; almost everything to the wife with several family heirlooms distributed equally among the siblings. No one seemed surprised, particularly pleased, or interested until Mark's name came up. With all eyes on Dobson, he presented Mark with a sealed envelope and said, "I suppose that only you and Howard know the contents. Mr. Goldstein asked only that you do the right thing." With that, Dobson closed his briefcase, spoke briefly with the widow and family, and left.

Everyone looked at Mark, expecting him to open the envelope and share the contents. Instead, he extended his condolences to the wife and family and made for the door. Just as he opened it to leave, one of two men were about to ring the bell. One was a distinguished looking white man accompanied by an even more distinguished looking Arab. Thinking Mark was answering the door in anticipation of his ringing the bell, the Arab man started to apologize and explain that he and his friend were longtime associates of Howard's from his diplomatic days and were there to pay their respects to the family. Mark did not respond, but left the door open.

Chapter Four
The Envelope and the Key

Howard's Asian wife's name was Asia (probably only her parents knew why). Mark could not stop thinking about her. She had shown genuine grief over the loss of her husband. His brothers and sisters, however, were not even pretending that they felt the loss.

Once in his car, Mark opened the envelope. Inside were several sheets of blank paper, a handwritten note, and a small flat key with the number 42 stamped on it. Mark guessed that the blank sheets were an effort to conceal the key from anyone handling the envelope. He began reading the note:

Mark, this key opens a locker I have at the YMCA. Inside, you'll find everything you need to make things right. Please take care that Asia is kept out of this.

Mark held the key in his hand, staring at it. He knew that his best option was to turn it, the letter, and the newspaper clippings over to the police and let them handle it. It was the simplest and most common-sense thing to do. He sat there, staring at the key and wondering why he wasn't doing it. He headed for home.

He wasn't home very long before his phone rang. "Mr. Brooks, this is Asia Goldstein."

"Mrs. Goldstein, I am so sorry—"

"Mr. Brooks, what do you know about my husband's death?"

"I'm not sure I understand…?"

"My husband did not commit suicide, and I think you know that."

"Mrs. Goldstein, I'm not sure I know what you're talking about."

"I know my husband had been acting strange for some time before his death, and not long after his death three men show up at my home who I have never seen or heard of, and one of them is included in his will!"

"Mrs. Goldstein, I can assure you I have no idea who those men were."

"And just what is your connection to my husband?"

"We met at a support group."

"A support group? Support for what?"

"Support for an addiction." Maybe being honest was the way to change the topic, or maybe make things worse.

"Howard stopped acting out years ago, all that was behind him. Are you saying he had a relapse?"

'Acting out', 'relapse'—clearly Mrs. Goldstein was familiar with sex addiction and now she knew Mark was too.

"Sometimes people just need a little support to help them get past a tough time."

"And you helped him so much he decided to put you in his will?"

"I'm not quite sure why he put me in his will." That was partially true.

"Those two men who came in after you, were they really diplomats or members of your support group?"

"I had never seen either of them before they came to your door."

"Mr. Brooks, just so you know, I am an attorney and a damn good one. I will get to the bottom of this, I promise you…I guess there's no point in asking you what was in the envelope Howard ·left you."

"I haven't opened it yet." Howard had asked him to keep her out of it.

"Will you please let me know if it's anything that will help me? If you were truly Howard's friend, you will do that."

"I will."

"Thank you."

With that she was gone, no goodbye. Mark replayed the conversation in his head. "She's a lawyer?" Just then, his phone rang again.

"Mrs.—"

"Is this Mark Brooks?"

"I'm sorry, yes, it is. Who is this?"

"My name is Fred Randolph. We met briefly at Howard's. Did I interrupt you? You seemed to be expecting someone else's call."

"No, that's fine. Who did you say you were?"

"Fred Randolph, a longtime friend of Howard's."

"What can I do for you, Mr. Randolph?"

"Please, call me Fred. Well, it seems that I had entrusted some very important papers with Howard for safekeeping that were not returned before he passed away. None of his brothers or sisters seemed to know anything about them. However, one of his sisters mentioned that you received an envelope?"

"Just a personal note from Howard."

"I see."

"Did you ask Mr. Dobson or Mrs. Goldstein?"

"Unfortunately, Mr. Dobson had already left and Mrs. Goldstein seemed too distraught to deal with matters of this sort. I'll call Mr. Dobson and check with Mrs. Goldstein at a better time."

"Is that all?"

"Certainly. I'll let you get back to your other call. Thank you."

It was obvious that Fred knew Mark had expected someone else when he answered his phone, and no doubt he suspected it was Mrs. Goldstein.

The fact that Fred had called Mark before he talked to Mrs. Goldstein about the missing "papers" was probably to eliminate Mark as someone who might have what he was looking for.

Fred had no idea that Mark knew about Howard's addiction and incarceration. No diplomat would trust Howard, a convicted felon, with any important diplomatic material. Fred was looking for something very important to him. If it had anything to do with that girl's death, he was probably desperate enough to do whatever was necessary to get it back.

Now, the question was whether to warn Mrs. Goldstein about Fred. He was unsure of what to do next. Then he remembered the key. Feeling his life was in danger, Howard could have given the key to his wife, or better yet, sent it to the police and let them find what was in the locker and take his revenge on Fred, but he didn't. He wanted Mark to find the locker and "do the right thing".

The downtown YMCA, like the rest of the inner city, had seen better days. Most residents and businesses had long ago left for the suburbs. What remained were those who couldn't leave, or wouldn't. The "Y" soldiered on, serving mostly youth clubs and inner-city swim and basketball teams as well as neighborhood social gatherings. Lockers could be rented for a small monthly fee and were mostly used as safe deposit boxes for those with no bank accounts.

No one stopped him as he walked past the empty reception desk to the area where the men's lockers were located. The lockers were the typical long metal ones converted from padlocks to key access. Mark found locker 42 and felt a rush as he opened it.

Chapter Five
The Locker

The locker contained a large duffel bag in the clothing area and a large cardboard cigar box· on the personal belongings shelf. Mark unzipped the duffel and discovered a note on top, "for Asia". The rest of the duffel was stuffed with stacks of bundled money. Hundreds of thousands worth of large denomination bills. What really caused his jaw to drop were the stacks of what Mark recognized from law school as corporate and Government Bearer Bonds.

Bearer Bonds are a type of unregistered debt security where no records were kept of the owner or the transactions involving ownership. Whoever physically held the bonds could legally cash them in at any time, no questions asked. Just at a glance, these bonds were worth millions.

Mark had to catch his breath before looking anxiously around to see if anyone had seen him open the bag. He zipped up the bag, took it out of the locker and sat it next to him on the bench. Anyone walking by would just assume it was his. He took the cigar box off the shelf. Inside were two VHS videotapes with no labels. The duffel was too heavy to carry with one hand so he slung it over his shoulder and carried the box of tapes under his arm as he walked past the still unmanned reception desk to his car.

The first thing that he needed to do was to find something he could use to view the tapes. After visiting several thrift shops, he was finally able to find a 19-inch Panasonic combo TV, VHS, and FM television. As he headed home, he wondered how he was going to broach the subject of the duffel bag and the money and bonds with Asia Goldstein. After all, it was hers, he had no intention of keeping any of it. Explaining how he came to have it, which he knew, or where it came from, which he didn't, would be a difficult conversation at the very least. Especially since Howard asked to keep her out of it.

It was dark by the time that he reached his apartment and he was glad for the end of a long day. As he put down the duffel and box to fumble for his keys, he noticed that his door was slightly ajar. He stepped back, his mind racing, not sure what to do. Suppose somebody was in there? Should he call the police? Or was it more likely he had just not closed the door completely when he left earlier? Convincing himself that this was the most likely scenario, Mark pushed open the door to his apartment and went inside.

As soon as he entered, he knew he had made a terrible mistake. His apartment was in shambles. The place had been ransacked. Most everything had been either tossed on the floor or broken. Nothing had been left untouched, and his computer was gone. A feeling of panic set in. It had to be Fred or some of the other "poker players". Most probably it was the money and bonds they were looking for, but why take his computer? They probably waited until he went out and then broke in, or worse yet, didn't care if he was home or not. Whatever the case, he could not stay here tonight. He didn't know quite what to do. Whoever it was might be coming back.

He packed the duffel and tapes into his car along with the TV and drove to the radio station. He felt somewhat safe at the station. There were people there during the day and he could lock the doors when he was there alone. The station had a small room in the back that the DJs and crews used for lounging and napping. There was also a kitchenette area with a refrigerator and microwave. Once there, the panic subsided a little and Mark felt somewhat comfortable in familiar surroundings. He turned his attention to the tapes.

What he saw left him horrified and sick to his stomach as he watched in disbelief.

The videos were made in several countries, Africa, India, Vietnam, and Eastern Europe. They showed a young Fred Randolph and several other men engaged in unimaginable acts of depravity with children as young as six, none older than twelve or thirteen. These men knew they were being filmed and even seemed to play to the camera. The faces of the men changed from country to country, but Fred was a constant; center stage in just about every scene of every tape, smiling while committing unspeakable acts on frightened, defenseless children.

Mark's addiction had been casual, consensual sex with women of age, often two or three simultaneously. Thank God and the Program that he was now "sober". He knew many members of his SAA group who were addicted to, and had gone to jail for just viewing child pornography. These men were actually committing the act._

It was10 pm, by the time Mark finished fast forwarding through the second tape. He was bone-tired and still had to prepare for his shift. He fought the urge to think about what to do next with the tapes and the duffel. He decided that sleep was his best option. He retired to the napping area. He sleep-walked his way through his time slot, hoping that his listeners couldn't tell how fatigued he was. The four hours felt like twelve. When the morning crew arrived, Mark hung around the lounge trying to make light conversation. Anything to keep from going home. Finding most people too busy to chat for long, he sat down with the station's copy of the morning newspaper.

It was on the second page, underneath the fold: "Local Attorney injured in home invasion. Silver City Attorney Ellis J. Dobson was severely beaten and robbed last evening by unknown assailants. Attorney Dobson was abducted from his home and taken to his office where police say the assault took place. The attorney's home and office both were ransacked, and computers and other papers taken. Police have no clues and no apparent motive. Attorney Dobson remains in Mercy General Hospital where doctors describe his condition as stable."

Mark put down the paper without finishing the article. Obviously, Fred and his associates were looking for the tapes and Dobson had been unlucky enough to be home when they came calling. If Dobson was beaten, it was most likely in an effort to find out if he had the tapes or knew anything about where they could be located. If Dobson truly didn't know what was in the envelope he gave Mark at the reading, or anything about the contents of the YMCA locker, then Fred now knew that too. That meant Mrs. Goldstein was probably next on their list and that he should warn her that she was in danger. That is if she had not already suffered a similar fate as Dobson.

Mark pulled out his cell phone and looked up Howard's number from the SAA "call list" for members. He was taken by surprise and fear when a man answered the phone.

"May I speak with Mrs. Goldstein please?" Mark tried to control his shaky voice. (Would robbers answer the phone?)

"Who's calling?"

He took a chance. "Attorney Mark Brooks. Mrs. Goldstein and I spoke earlier."

"This is Detective Dick Price. Mrs. Goldstein can't come to the phone right now."

"Is she okay? Has something happened to her?"

"She's fine. Was this about the burglary at her home last evening?"

"No, it was a legal matter."

"Well, you will have to call back later. We're in the middle of an investigation."

"I understand. Will you tell her I called, and that I will call back later?"

"Yeah."

"Thanks."

Dick Price was a veteran homicide detective. He had received many awards and commendations throughout a long career. With the rise of a younger, more progressive regime of police Commissioners Detective Price's old school methods and tactics were now frowned upon, and he was eventually reassigned to the Non-Violent Crimes Unit. A last humiliation before forced retirement.

Still, his old-school instincts were there and intact, and they told him something was not right with the burglary at the Goldstein house. The Goldsteins weren't rich, and the intruder seemed to have gone through the house on a fishing expedition. They were looking for something in particular they hoped to find there. Mrs. Goldstein's husband had died recently under what she considered suspicious circumstances.

Plus, although it was common police knowledge that burglars often target the homes of the recently deceased, they took the usual items: TVs, stereos, jewelry, money, etc. All of which were left untouched, except for the missing computers. Most importantly, they wouldn't pick a house where the surviving spouse might be at home.

Mark was glad that Mrs. Goldstein was safe and that the police were there to keep her that way. He wondered if she had mentioned her suspicions about her husband's death to the detective. He would give the police a couple of hours to clear out and then try to contact her again.

He spent the next hour or so preparing for his radio show. He hoped to make it up to his listeners that he knew felt cheated by his less than usual performance last morning. He was just wrapping up the playlist when his phone rang.

"Mr. Brooks this is Asia Goldstein. You wanted to talk to me?"

"Yes, I was going to call back. How did you get my cell number?"

"I'm a member of the Bar Association. You listed your home and cell number in the directory." A mistake he immediately regretted when he did it.

"Look, we have to talk."

"Is this about my husband or the break-in?"

"Both. Mrs. Goldstein, I wasn't being completely truthful with you when we last spoke."

Mark stumbled as he tried to tell her about everything. His conversation with Howard, the envelope with the key, the tapes and the money and bonds. He told her about his apartment also being burglarized. He also told her about Ellis Dobson and Fred Randolph. She didn't interrupt his rambling. She was so silent that Mark began to think he had lost the connection.

"I'm sorry to put all of this on you, but with your house being burglarized too and what happened to Dobson, I thought you might be in danger."

Silence.

"Mrs. Goldstein?"

"Where can I meet you, Mr. Brooks? We have to talk."

Chapter Six
Mrs. Goldstein

Mark suggested a popular restaurant downtown where there would be people around plus secluded booths allowing for privacy. He arrived at the La Petit Chateau at the appointed time only to find Mrs. Goldstein already seated with half a glass of wine.

"Sorry, I needed a drink."

"It's okay, I could use one myself. Mrs. Goldstein, I—"

"Call me Asia."

"Thank you, and I'm Mark."

"Mark, before you say anything, you need to hear what I have to say. I need to see those tapes."

"Shouldn't we just turn them over to the police? They don't need to know about the money and bonds."

"It's not about the money and bonds."

"You don't want to see the tapes, believe me."

"You think they're too shocking? Something I haven't seen before? There is nothing on those tapes that I have not witnessed or experienced."

Mark leaned forward and listened, spellbound, as Asia told her story.

Her real name was Nhu. She never had a last name or knew if she had any family. She had been brought up in a brothel in Vietnam; a brothel specializing in catering to the needs of men seeking the satisfaction of sexual contact with prepubescent girls and boys. Once the children were too old to be "useful", they were either put out on the street or sold as slaves to work as nannies, maids, or worse. Nhu had only been kept around because she was very good with the younger children, able to keep them calm, treat them when they were sick, and tend to any injuries they received. She was a surrogate mother at sixteen.

She knew the man who ran the brothel only as Raul. He was of Spanish descent, but spoke fluent French, English, and Vietnamese. Rumor had it that his family had been in Vietnam since the French occupation as major rice exporters and hoteliers. They had survived and prospered in the aftermath of Den Bien Phu and the U.S. Vietnam war. The family had other business outside Vietnam and Raul traveled abroad a lot, sometimes gone for weeks at a time. However, when he was there you could sense the tension and fear in everyone. Servants and workers coward and held their heads low. Children scurried out of his sight. Those who failed to please him were never seen at the compound again.

Once she was twelve or thirteen and considered "past her prime", she was never allowed to see the men who came to visit "Raul's Resort Hotel and Casino" to "see" the children. Raul would sometimes bring her to his suite as she became older, but at sixteen, she was now past the age to be of any interest to him.

That's where Howard came into the picture. She had seen him on occasion over the years with Raul, but he had never touched her. She had served him tea as he and Raul discussed business in French.

Then one day, without notice, Raul told her to gather what little she had and leave the compound with Howard. Her worse fear was being realized. She was being sold. She expected that she would now be subjected to more of the torment she had endured when she was young; the pain and humiliation she was no longer willing to accept. If it came to that, she was prepared to take her own life.

Instead, Howard treated her with a kindness and gentleness that she had never imagined. He took no liberties and provided her with transport out of Vietnam to India, where he enrolled her in an exclusive American school for diplomats and expatriates under the name Asia Goldstein, his niece, the orphaned daughter of a deceased brother.

Howard saw her whenever his schedule allowed. When he came to visit, he was always alone. His government contacts eventually made it possible for her to enter the United States on a temporary visa. Shortly thereafter, when she was of age, they were married; a marriage of convenience in order to give her permanent citizenship.

She had graduated college and got her law degree from Georgetown University in Washington D.C. Her practice, such as it was, was devoted to representing children and their families in lawsuits against pedophiles: priests, Scout leaders, teachers, coaches, etc. Her childhood and her marriage to Howard left her uniquely qualified.

Despite her zeal for seeing those who abused children and young adults held accountable and punished for their crimes against the innocent, she had steadfastly stood by Howard through his trial, conviction, and time in prison. She was the one who got him to his first SAA meeting and kept him going until they both felt he had the tools necessary to cope with his addiction. He had not "acted out" in years.

Mark felt compelled, in light of Asia's story, to make it clear that although he was a member of SAA, his addiction had nothing to do with children. He also was compelled to tell her that Howard had originally contacted him for legal advice. He wasn't sure if she believed him or not.

"I understand your passion, but why view the tapes and bring up all that hurt?"

"I need to see if someone is on those tapes."

"You said you didn't recognize Fred Randolph when he called at your house?"

"No, I was kept away when the clients came. Mr. Randolph is not the man I'm looking for. I need to see if Raul is on those tapes. If he is, Fred Randolph is not the one we need to be worried about."

Chapter Seven
Price and Artest

Dick Price stared at the no smoking sign on the wall opposite his office door, went inside, leaned back in his chair, lit his cigar, and blew smoke toward the ceiling vent. He had his ever-present cigar in his right hand and his ever-present Styrofoam cup of black coffee in his left. His partner Susan Artest sat across from him.

"What do you think about coincidences Artest?"

"Like what?"

"Like the Goldstein case."

"Not sure what you're talking about?"

"Like Mrs. Goldstein's husband was a convicted sex offender, yet she sues sex offenders for a living. Then, right after her husband dies, under what she thinks are suspicious circumstances, her home is burglarized by an individual or individuals looking for something on their computers. Then we learn that the lawyer who presided over the reading of the will is taken from his home and beaten severely while both his office and home computers are also taken. To top it off, another attorney who happens to be named as a beneficiary in the will just happens to call her minutes after her home is burglarized. I'm just saying, what are the odds?"

"With crime and attorneys, I'd say pretty high."

"Seriously Artest, I tell you we're missing something here."

"So, I'm guessing you want to talk to these two attorneys? You want to talk to Mrs. Goldstein again too?"

"You got something better to do?"

Price and Artest arrived at the home of Ellis Dobson just as the home care nurse was leaving. As she let them in, they could see Dobson sitting in a wheelchair, his left arm in a cast. On closer inspection, they could see he had two black eyes and several stitches in his upper and lower lips. His face showed signs of severe bruising.

"Mr. Dobson, my name is Detective Price, and this here is my partner Detective Artest."

"I've already told your colleagues everything I remember about the abduction."

"That's not why we're here. We would like to talk specifically about the events leading up to your abduction."

"I'm not sure I understand?"

"We are investigating a burglary that took place right about the same time as your home invasion involving a client of yours and we think they might be connected."

"I'm still not sure…"

"Mrs. Howard Goldstein is a client of yours, isn't she?"

"Her husband was."

"Well, her home was burglarized right after your encounter. We think she was fortunate not to be home at the time. The only things taken were her and her husband's computers. We understand those are the only two things taken from your home and office. Is that true?"

Dobson restated what he had told the other detectives;' that his abductors were definitely looking for something they thought he had hidden somewhere.

They made no mention of the Goldsteins. They just kept saying, "You know what we're looking for, tell us where it is and we will leave."

Dobson said that the reading of the will was non-eventful, no big reveal, no hidden assets or family secrets and no bickering among the widow and the family members. When asked if he remembered anything that seemed at all out of the ordinary, he said it was unusual for another attorney to be present that none of the family knew, and for that attorney to receive a bequest from the deceased. A sealed envelope along with Howard's admonition to "do the right thing".

Another thing also felt out of place. As he was leaving, he saw two men parked in an expensive car outside the Goldstein house. They appeared to be having a heated argument. He might have dismissed it except one of the men was an Arab.

"And in today's world, you tend to take notice of an angry Arab."

Mark and Asia did not order dinner. Instead, they both ordered several drinks during the evening. Mark agreed to Asia's request to see the tapes, but it would have to be at the station. He had no intention of returning to his apartment or going to the burglarized Goldstein house. She asked where he was staying since he couldn't go home. It was then that it dawned on him that he could not stay at the station indefinitely. It wouldn't take Fred Randolph and his associates long to find out where he worked and being at the station was no guarantee of safety considering he would often have to be there alone, and at some point he would have to venture out.

"I haven't found a permanent place yet."

"You'll need some money then, to get yourself set up."

"I just need a place to lay my head without waiting for someone to break down the door."

"Why don't you use the money you found in the locker and get yourself a place out of the city? Somewhere you can keep a low profile."

"The money and bonds are yours, or somebody's, I couldn't—"

"From what you told me, there's enough in that bag that no one would notice if some were missing."

Mark had to agree that the money was there and that getting out of the city to parts unknown was probably his best option. He'd clear out of the station right after his shift and live in a motel until he found suitable accommodations. That also meant he would have to leave his job at the station for a while to feel completely safe.

He had just finished telling Joe Stanton, the station manager, how he needed to take some extended vacation time immediately to handle some very important family business. Joe wasn't having any of it. He was not prepared for a sudden absence of one of his most popular DJs for an indefinite time. What was he supposed to do in Mark's time slot, play Muzak. The station had no one available to fill in and no time to hire a replacement. It finally came down to this. If Mark was intent on leaving under these circumstances, then there was no need for him to return.

Joe was a good man, a good boss, and a good friend. Mark apologized for letting him down and left the office to gather his things. Joe just sat there shaking his head, dumbfounded.

Mark began gathering his things from his locker. It would take two trips to his car because of his personal things, the TV, duffel bag and tapes. He put his personal items in a backpack, put it on, took up the bag and the tapes and headed for the elevator. He walked past the stunned and puzzled looks of his coworkers. All eyes were on him, but no one said anything; no questions, no good-luck handshakes. What had Joe told them? The office door was closed and the blinds drawn. Mark felt even worse as he passed by. He wanted at least to look in and acknowledge their friendship.

He was about to enter the elevator when he heard Joe call his name and wave him back to the office. He'd get that chance for a goodwill farewell after all.

When he walked into the office, he knew this wasn't about saying goodbye to his friend. The man and woman seated around Joe's desk were obviously police.

"Mark, these are Detectives Price and Artest…They've asked to have a word with you."

With that, Joe walked out of the office, closing the door as he left. Everyone had watched as the detectives went into Joe's office. No wonder no one wanted to be seen shaking his hand.

Detective Artest broke the awkward silence. "Would you mind taking a seat, Mr. Brooks?"

The only chair left, other than Joe's, was a straight back located in the corner. Mark continued to stand. "Can I ask what this is about?"

Artest replied: "We'd just like a few minutes of your time. It won't take long. Please, take a seat."

Mark moved toward the straight back, put the backpack, duffel, and box down beside it, and took a seat on the edge.

"We had officers knock on your door several times this week. You haven't been home."

"Yeah, I'm in the process of moving."

"Oh, are you leaving town?"

Mark's attention was focused on the male detective, who was clearly the senior in rank of the two. He said nothing. Instead, he kept his eyes fixed on Mark's.

"Mr. Brooks?"

"I'm sorry, what did you say?"

"Are you leaving town?"

"Not sure, maybe. Why is it you said you needed to talk to me?"

"That's sort of sudden, isn't it? To quit your job and move out of your apartment?"

"Yes, well, I have pressing personal business I need to attend to and I need some space and time to work things through."

Mark could not stop thinking how utterly bizarre this whole scene was. Here he was, being questioned by two police detectives with a box of child pornography and a duffel bag full of millions of dollars of currency at his feet. If he were not scared to death, he might have burst out laughing.

He was brought abruptly back to focus by Artest's question. "Mr. Brooks, how well do you know the Goldsteins?"

"I knew Mr. Goldstein."

"And how well do you know Ellis Dobson?"

"I don't. I just met him at the reading."

"Were you aware that both Mrs. Goldstein and Mr. Dobson were victims of break-ins following the reading?"

"I read about Attorney Dobson in the newspaper, and I talked to a detective at Mrs. Goldstein's, which left me thinking that some type of incident had taken place at her home also."

"Anything unusual happen at your home?"

"No. Are you saying that the two break-ins are connected?"

"We're looking into it. You got a bequest at the reading, didn't you?"

"Yes, I did, a personal note from Mr. Goldstein."

"And how well did you say you knew Mr. Goldstein?"

"We had become acquainted within the last year or so."

"Well enough acquainted that he would put you in his will?"

"As I said, it was just a personal note. Is that all? I need to be going."

"I understand, just one other question. How well do you know the Arab man and his friend who came to the reading?"

"I don't. I just saw them as I was leaving. Is that it?"

"Yes, thank you for your time. I can see that you're anxious to get your things and get out of here. If we need to talk again, where can we reach you?"

Mark picked up the backpack, strapped it on and picked up the box and duffel. Each of which now felt like they weighed a hundred pounds. He gave the detectives the name of the motel he was staying at and left the office.

"What do you think?" asked Artest.

"He's lying."

"What makes you think that?"

"For starters, he's a lawyer."

Chapter Eight
Raul

Raul's father was from Nice, France, originally from Spain. He was a former French Foreign Legion officer who defected and went to Vietnam to help Ho Chi Minh and General Giap train the Viet Minh in their fight against the Japanese in World War Two.

After the war, he stayed on to fight for Vietnam's independence from France. His actions made him infamous in France and celebrated in Vietnam.

After he helped defeat the French in the battle of Dien Bien Phu, he was granted land in appreciation for his service. He cultivated rice and eventually began to provide luxury accommodations at his hotel for wealthy businessmen and tourists.

From the outset, it was said the former French officer brought in French prostitutes rather than mix with the Vietnamese women. It was a debate as to whether he did this out of prejudice or in deference to Vietnamese social customs frowning on interracial relationships that could produce offspring.

Raul was born in Saigon. His mother's name was Collette. She was the Madam the former Legionnaire brought over from France to run his brothel. Raul's father was Antonio Hernandez. Antonio and Colette were never married but everyone knew that she was special to him and gave her the respect due a wife.

Raul was the only child of the couple and grew up with all the affection of both parents, especially his mother. She doted on him and refused him nothing. As a result, Raul became a very vain, callous, and selfish youth. He could be cruel, bordering on vicious, whenever he felt the need to assert his position as heir apparent to his father. Especially to those he imagined behind his back referred to him as "The bastard son of the whore".

Raul's father had been wounded in the battle of Dien Bien Phu. A wound that left him in constant pain that increased the older he got. Eventually, his heath declined, to the point where his heart gave out. His mother, after the death of his father, expanded the hotel business beyond just serving tourist and expatriates. As the hotel's reputation grew, she was the first to notice that many of the visitors had a taste for the exotic. She made it known that the Hernandez properties spared nothing when it came to catering to the wishes of their guests. The hotel gained a well-earned reputation for supplying "those things most difficult to acquire".

Under his mother's guidance, the rice and "hospitality" business grew, and other financial holdings were added to the portfolio. Collette proved a formidable CEO with a reputation for doing whatever was necessary to get what she wanted. She ran her businesses with an iron fist and Raul was the club in that fist. There were rampant rumors, whispers only, of blackmail, kidnappings, assaults, and even murder. However, nothing was ever spoken aloud.

Raul was devoted to his mother and well suited as her enforcer. As Collette grew older more and more of the day-to-day business operations fell to him, his business accomplishments exceeded that of his mother. Under Raul most of the family businesses were now legitimate enterprises. The drug trafficking, cargo hijacking and other criminal pursuits were all but gone.

However, the root business of the sex trade, his mother's profession from the beginning, never waned. It went international, exclusively dedicated to the sexual exploitation of children. For rent or for sale.

Chapter Nine
The Gates Begin to Open

It was now obvious to Mark that the radio station was probably not the best place for Asia to view the tapes. That was minor compared to the need for him to quickly find a place out of the reach of both Fred Randolph and the police.

He spent the week after they met at the restaurant searching the suburbs and surrounding area for a suitable place to move. For the first time in his life he did not have to consider price in deciding where he wanted to live. He mailed the remainder of the money on his apartment lease plus damages to his former landlord, including the penalty for breaking the lease. He included a letter saying that any useable content of his apartment could either sold, donated to charity, or thrown away. He posted the letter and money from just over the state line as a measure of precaution.

The events of the last few days hit him all at once. In the blink of an eye, his life had turned upside down. Nothing would ever be the same. He had lost his home, his job, and his personal sense of safety. He was literally hiding from the police and persons willing to hurt him; plus, he was rich.

Mark and his real estate agent, Sam Arnold had been driving around looking at houses for two days. Both men were feeling the frustration. They were driving in silence and just about to call quits when, in desperation, Sam spoke up.

"Look, we've seen just about everything I've got and I'm still not sure I know what you're looking for."

"I'll know it when I see it."

"Well, I say we call it a day. Maybe we can talk some more in the office before going out tomorrow. Maybe I can get a better feel for what you're looking for."

"That's fine."

The two men drove on in a tense silence. Feeling he was losing his client, Sam made one last effort. "Look, I know we both are tired, but if you've got a little more time, there's another place I could show you, but it's a little bit of a drive from here."

Mark was thinking how he could cancel tomorrow and find another agent. "Sure, why not."

The "little drive" turned out to be forty-five minutes, out to an area Mark did not recognize as Silver City. He was just about to protest when Sam made an abrupt turn.

"It's just down this road. It's not fancy, but it's quite comfortable, and you can't beat the privacy."

The house was an odd looking structure, like someone couldn't make up their mind whether they wanted a cabin or a cottage. It sat alone in the middle of nowhere surrounded by a field and some dense large oak trees. Inside, it had two floors, two small bedrooms, a spacious kitchen, a single bath, a large common area, and an office.

"Well, what do you think?"

"Can you get cell service out here?"

"That is a problem. It's spotty. Depends on where you're standing."

"I like it."

"Great! I can probably get you a great deal. Take a look around."

Mark had already made up his mind. Despite its odd appearance, the location gave him a certain sense of peace. The word sanctuary came to mind.

"No, I'm ready to sign the papers. I don't need to see anymore. I'll pay the asking price."

"But you haven't seen the best part."

"What else is there?"

"Follow me."

Mark watched as Sam slipped out the back door and underneath the porch, reached down and pulled open a hatch.

"What is this, a root cellar?"

"Bomb shelter."

"Bomb shelter?"

"Of sorts; come, take a look."

The two men climbed down the narrow set of stairs into the room underneath the house. The place was surprisingly large. It had a bed, a shower with curtains, well stocked shelves of food, and a decent bathroom. The "living room" was small, but large enough.

"It has an excellent ventilation system. You could stay down here for months."

"Who built this place?"

"The guy was, what do you call it, a survivalist, waiting for Armageddon I guess."

"Then why is he selling it now?"

"He isn't, died in a car crash. Gives you a whole new perspective on survivalist, huh?"

Mark could see how someone waiting for the collapse of civilization would choose a place like this. Out in a space like this, surrounded by a clearing that gave you a good 360-degree field of vision so as not to be surprised by anyone approaching the house, and a hidden escape hatch if all else failed.

Chapter Ten
Fred and Amir

Fred Randolph and Amir Raji sat in Fred's hotel room at the Ritz Carlton. They were trying to figure out their next move, and time was running out. They were now sure that Ellis Dobson did not have the tapes or knew anything about their contents. They also knew that neither Asia Goldstein nor Mark Brooks had the tapes at their homes or on their computers, and they knew that Mrs. Goldstein had not seen the tapes before the reading or she would have recognized Fred when she saw him.

Amir: "So, what now? Raul's guys hacked the computers and there's nothing there. Our hired muscle came up empty too."

"Look Amir, they have to be out there somewhere. Howard probably kept them as his insurance. The fact that they haven't surfaced means either he didn't tell anybody and they've gone to the grave with him, or someone has them and doesn't know it."

"How could anyone be so stupid as to allow this stuff to be taped?"

"It was a different time, people wanted souvenirs, keepsakes. The spotlight wasn't anything like it is now. Hell, most people didn't know we existed."

"We need to have Raul's guys have a talk with the wife and this Brooks guy like we did with Dobson. That's the only way to be sure."

"And you think the police won't make a connection? No, we need to lay low and see what happens. For all we know, Howard has them in some safe deposit box somewhere under another name, or whatever, and until the bank or whoever notifies the next of kin, we're safe."

"How will we know when or if that happens?"

"Good question."

"You know he won't wait. Sooner rather than later, Raul will decide to tie up all loose ends, and that will include us."

"So that means we better figure this out soon."

Fred Randolph was a career diplomat who had quickly risen in the ranks. Along the way he had made many influential friends and contacts, both in and out of government. He had received and given many favors over the years and was known as a man who could be trusted to keep secrets.

He was the only child of wealthy parents who pampered him and groomed him for success. He was a natural athlete and scholar. His father wanted him to go into politics. His mother saw him taking over her father's business in international finance. It was no surprise when Fred entered Yale University to study both political science and international studies. After Yale, he received a master's degree in International Affairs from Columbia University, keeping alive the dreams of both his parents.

For all his hopes of being the youngest Senator in U.S. history or the youngest billionaire in international finance, Fred's career in the diplomat corps began to falter. Bogged down by his inability to get along with people he believed were inferior intellectually or lacked the proper social standing, regardless of their position or authority. He became smug, resentful, and prone to bouts of depression as his aspirations waned and his career stalled.

It was during those times of depression that his sexual obsession would take control. He had always been fascinated with the human body, both male and female. As an athlete, he was familiar with seeing men without their clothes and quietly admired the adolescent physique. He didn't consider himself homosexual since he was equally aroused by the sight of the scantily clad young girls at his school. He idolized youth and its innocence. When he was older, he still had those feelings of fascination even though his own youthful appearance was gone. Too many diplomatic functions with their extravagant meals and drink had taken a toll.

It was a complex combination of alternating boredom and stress that had drawn him to pornography, first as a way to escape either or both and second as a weapon to ward off the debilitating depression.

Fred discovered that his adolescent fantasies could be realized in faraway places where people with wealth and influence did not have to waste their time looking at pictures.

Amir Raji was supposedly a distant cousin to the Dubai royal family. He had attended some of the most prestigious schools in both the Middle East and the United States but held no degree of any kind. He was very handsome and had a legitimate reputation as a playboy. He enjoyed being considered one of the world's most eligible bachelors during his youth. As he grew older, his celebrity suffered as rumors spread of his penchant for young girls and the paparazzi began to dog his every move in search of a smoking gun. He eventually dropped out of the social scene and left the United States and Europe for less visible surroundings.

Amir had met Fred during his playboy days, when he was a frequent guest at diplomatic affairs and dinner parties where the "who's who" of the rich and famous were invited to socialize with the politically powerful. Over the years, they had spent many an after dinner evening drinking and searching the most undesirable parts of cities looking for a singular entertainment. Both men had become acutely aware of the other's taste and together they pursued their passion, fueled by Amir's easy access to money and Fred's access to those people capable of fulfilling their appetite—at a price.

All had gone well until that night when everything went wrong. Nothing like that had ever happened before. Amir was scared. He was always a follower, allowing others to do the planning and the thinking. He was simply the money man. He had no idea what to do now. He needed Fred to figure something out. All he knew for certain was their lives depended on it.

Chapter Eleven
Gotcha

"How do you like my new home?"

"Where the hell are we?"

"I honestly don't know, somewhere near the outskirts of the city, I think."

Mark gave Asia a quick tour of his new home. As he showed her the safe room he began to tell her the story of the previous owner. Asia interrupted when she noticed there was a small door, barely visible, on the floor next to the bed.

"Is that where you keep the money and the tapes?"

"I had no idea that was there."

"What do you suppose he kept in there?"

"He died suddenly, so whatever it is, it's still in there; if the real estate people didn't take it."

Mark knelt down and opened the door. Inside he found two handguns and an assault rifle with enough ammunition to fend off a small army of invaders. He and Asia just stared at the weapons. Neither was familiar with firearms and were at a loss as to what to do about the discovery.

"Just get rid of them."

"How? You can't just throw them in the trash can."

"Then put them back and lock that door."

Mark replaced the weapons and the two left the room. He got some logs from the stack outside to light the fireplace to take the chill off inside the house. He poured himself and Asia a glass of wine to do the same. Then he put the first tape into the VCR.

For the second time since his interview with the detectives, Mark experienced that feeling of the absurd. How bizarre was this? Here he was sitting next to a warm fire sharing a glass of wine, watching pornography next to a woman who embodied all of his sexual fantasies. All without any sense of sensuality.

Instead, he felt extremely uncomfortable, wanting to fast forward through the most explicit, disturbing parts of the tape. Asia insisted on viewing everything in real time. Mark excused himself on the pretense of pouring himself another glass of wine. He could not sit there another minute, another second. His absence went without notice or comment from Asia.

"Stop the tape!"

"What?"

"You have the remote, put it on hold."

Mark fumbled to recover the remote from the kitchen counter. "What is it?"

"Look!" Asia pointed to the extreme right corner of the TV. There, almost out of camera range, was a man who obviously didn't know he was being filmed. "Gotcha."

"Is that Raul?"

"Howard got him on film. Brilliant!"

"What does that mean?"

"It means that there is proof that this man is involved in the sexual exploitation of children and now he's going to pay for it."

Chapter Twelve
Revelations

Raul was growing impatient. He had not heard from Fred in a while and was beginning to have doubts about whether Fred and Amir were up to the task. He had provided them the muscle and computer expertise they requested and had hoped this problem could be resolved quickly. They had already bungled things by allowing one of his girls to die at their hands and panicking to the point of getting rid of the girl's body and eliminating Howard without using his people. Goldstein was dead before he could talk to the police but without recovering any evidence that he might have shared incriminating him or his "clients". How stupid could these people be to keep evidence of their crimes as souvenirs?

Fred never said exactly what it was that Howard had that could be used against him, but Raul suspected it had to be pictures of Fred with children.

Raul knew not to have keepsakes. He was a purveyor of the forbidden, but rarely indulged in the practice himself. His tryst with underage girls were very private affairs with carefully selected "partners" known for their devotion and loyalty to him. They had all been "willing". He prided himself on the fact he had never forced himself on anyone. Never acknowledging the fact that these were children.

Maybe it was time to take control of the situation and cut any potential ties to himself. Who knows what secrets Howard Goldstein might have hidden somewhere? Goldstein knew Raul, he knew him well. His name might be in some diary, notebook or whatever. People like Fred were oblivious to the implications of failing to take all the necessary precautions to hide their activities and safeguard their identity. If those two idiots were ever picked up by the police, they would immediately roll on him and everybody else.

The more he thought about it, the more convinced he became that there was too much personal risk for him to leave this to amateurs. He summoned his most trusted servant and confidant. A man who had been at his side since he was a child. The man his mother had early on specifically designated as his protector. A man who had proven time and again over the years that he was willing and capable of performing whatever task Raul set before him.

Johan Stannis was a big, powerful man. He stood over six and a half feet tall and weighed somewhere in the neighborhood of 275lbs. His strength was legendary. Raul called Johan and told him they were going to the U.S.

Fred and Amir drove past Mark's old apartment again. There was still no sign of anyone being home and he wasn't answering his phone.

Amir: "Maybe we should ask the landlord or one of the neighbors. Maybe they know where he is, or maybe where he works?"

"Too risky. I got some local government contacts looking into him. If he's been involved with the city in any way, they will let me know."

"What are the chances of that?"

"Him being involved in the city or them letting me know?"

"Both."

"These guys work at City Hall. They can access police records, work licenses, permits of any kind. If this guy works in the city or has had a run-in with the law, they've got a good chance of finding him. He has to make a living. They can also keep tabs on the police investigation into the death of that girl without raising suspicions or involving us."

"And what did you tell them you needed this information for?"

"We're checking him out for security reasons. He's applying for a job in government and we want to find out as much as we can about him from multiple sources. We understand the police are looking at him as a person of interest in a burglary case. Anyway, cruising around here isn't getting us anywhere."

"What about the wife? I still say she's the one most likely to have it."

"Yeah, maybe, but with her house just being burglarized, we should probably back off for now. No need to raise the suspicions of the police more than they probably are, what with what happened with the lawyer and all."

Price and Artest were having lunch at their desks. Artest was having a salad with a bottle of water. Price was wolfing down his second double-decker hamburger between gulps of a 64 once "Big Thirsty" Dr. Pepper.

Patrolman James Jones approached the office wondering if he should wait until the two finished lunch. He was due back on duty in a few minutes, so he didn't have a lot of time. Price noticed him hovering around the door and looking anxious.

"What is it, kid?"

Jones knew of Price's reputation within the department. Most officers felt he had been given a raw deal. He was one of the last real detectives left on the force and he envied Artest being his partner. Jones tried to sound assertive.

"You guys still looking into that Goldstein thing with the lawyer?"

Artest: "What?"

"The case where both the victim and her lawyer were robbed."

Price: "Yea, you got something?"

"Well, I heard that you were looking for a late model car with two guys, one of them an Arab?"

Artest: "You found them?"

"Maybe. We got a call from a woman complaining about a suspicious car roaming her neighborhood, two men inside. One of them was an Arab. It was the Arab that made her call."

Artest stopped mid-chew, and Price felt the Dr. Pepper go up his nose when Jones told them the location where the car was spotted.

"I knew it!" Dick said.

They got the name of the complainant and Price made the unusual gesture of patting the patrolman on the back.

"Good job, son. What did you say your name was again?"

"Jones sir, James Jones."

"I'll remember that."

Jones left the office on a high. Praise from Price was a rarity, and he knew the man wouldn't forget him.

Mrs. Amanda Peabody (Amanda "Seebody" as she was known in the neighborhood) was an eighty-four-year-old widowed, retired schoolteacher who spent her days sitting by her front window watching the comings and goings of her neighbors. You needed to be sure you kept your blinds and curtains closed since she was not averse to peering into any house or apartment that failed to do so. On occasion, her nosiness had proved invaluable as when the neighborhood had been plagued with a series of muggings. She was able to give a complete and accurate description of the culprits to the police. Her mind was sharp, her eyesight keen. She was the perfect witness.

Amanda told the detectives that the car she saw was a late model Lincoln Continental, dark blue. The license plates, front and back, appeared to be obscured on purpose. The two middle-aged men inside appeared to be "casing" the apartment building across the street. When asked about Mark Brooks, she confessed she did not know the man, but knew he kept odd hours and that he had recently moved out without taking any of his possessions. In fact, the landlord had a yard sale to "try to get rid of the junk".

Mark's landlord had half-expected the police to contact him again. He wasn't expecting detectives.

"I knew it was either the law or one of these gangs he was running from." Gangs had recently invaded some of the nearby communities. Several bystanders had been wounded as each one vied to control more territory. The whole city was on edge and not quite sure how to deal with the problem. The police were just beginning to form a gang task force in order to calm people's fears.

"You say the place was trashed?" Artest asked.

"Oh yeah, just about every piece of furniture was damaged. He said I could sell what I could and give everything else to charity. There wasn't much left to do either. He paid up his contract and damages to the apartment and that's the last I heard from him."

"Did he say anything about what happened when he paid you?"

"Didn't see him, he sent the money and instructions in the mail. It was postmarked out of state."

The detectives thanked him and walked back to the car.

"You were right; he was lying. But why would he not call the police in the first place and then lie about it when he had the chance to tell us when we interviewed him?"

"Because there is a hell of a lot more going on here than a string of burglaries. The only person involved in this thing that seems to be covering up is this Brooks guy."

"Are you sure about that? They're all lawyers."

Price handed the keys to the car to Artest. He sat in the passenger seat with his head back and his eyes closed. It was several minutes before he spoke.

"Let's go over this again. We got this registered pedophile who dies suddenly and suspiciously according to the wife. His wife is Asian-born—"

"What's that got to do with it?"

"Maybe nothing. Just hear me out. At the reading, three strangers show up, one of them another lawyer, is left a mysterious envelope the contents of which no one knows but him and the deceased. Mind you, with the admonition to do the right thing. The other two strangers, one of which is an Arab, are seen arguing in their car just before entering the house. Later that same evening, the deceased house is robbed but only their computers are taken. One lawyer is beaten to a pulp with both his home and office robbed but only his computers are taken.

"The other lawyer's apartment is ransacked, but he chooses to keep it a secret. Meanwhile, this Arab guy and his companion are staking out his apartment. It's got to be that envelope! These guys are after that envelope."

"But they weren't the ones who beat up the attorney."

"Hired muscle. Based on the car and their description, these are people of means. They won't get their hands dirty."

"So, the envelope is what led to all this?"

"The envelope and this Brooks guy. I'm willing to bet that the pedophile gave him something that could land the Arab and his friend in jail, and this lawyer is either in on it or running for his life."

"The wife?"

"Don't know yet. My gut tells me this thing has an international angle."

"That's quite a stretch."

"Yeah, maybe, but I betcha this all has something to do with the pedophile's sex conviction or the sex trade. Do me a favor; when we get back to the station, check with homicide and the sex crimes unit and see what you can find around the time of this Goldstein guy's death."

"Aren't we the non-violent crimes police? Where are you going with this?"

"Don't know. Right now, I'm just curious."

Bill Patterson and Buzz Peterson were veteran homicide detectives, neither of whom was enamored with the idea of female detectives, or women on the force period for that matter. However, they knew Dick Price and held him with the utmost respect. It was the only reason they agreed to talk to Artest.

They had been working the case of the girl found dead in the woods for a while now, and so far were coming up empty. Buzz was the lead detective on the case.

"No I.D. of any kind, but judging by her clothes, dental work, and lack of U.S. vaccinations, she probably came out of Eastern Europe. She was well-nourished but showed signs of physical and sexual abuse. Some healed bones, scarring and tearing of the vaginal and anal area. This poor girl had been through hell."

"How does a young girl like that get into the U.S.? Do you think she was here for domestic or field work?"

"Not likely, too young. Plus, her hands were soft and smooth, no sign of hard work. In fact, except for the obvious mistreatment, she was pretty well taken care of. Her clothing and dental work were testament to that."

Bill Paterson spoke up, "Our best guess is she was part of a sex trafficking ring. Smuggled into the country, and most likely not by herself. Somewhere, there are more like her. Something went wrong, who knows what, and she died and was dumped like garbage. Could be she was the lucky one."

"What's Dick's interest in homicide anyway?" Buzz interrupted. It irked Artest that that he didn't afford her the courtesy of acknowledging that both she and Price might be interested, or that she was asking out of her own interest.

People just assumed that Dick was the detective and she was little more than his secretary.

"I got a hunch that the case we're working may have some connection."

She knew that Dick would not be offended by her taking some credit. Since being assigned as his partner (a form of departmental punishment for his lack of respect for the establishment), he had grown to respect her and on occasion given her one of those rare pats on the back and a "good job, Detective".

"*YOU* got a hunch?" Buzz was regretting giving this woman the time of day. "Don't you guys work non-violent? Is Dick working homicide now?"

"It's a burglary case," she said, realizing immediately that she may have overstepped.

"A burglary case?" Buzz asked, half laughing, half serious.

This could be good. If they thought this came from Dick, they just might get interested enough to take their case more seriously, ask more questions, dig a little bit deeper. Believing it was her idea just made it sound comical to them.

"Thanks for the info guys. Really appreciate it."

"Yeah, anything to help. Tell Dick we feel his pain." The smirk on Bill's face was barely hidden.

Artest had to admire the fact that Price had figured out this connection with little more than cop instinct. What if this turned into something big? Nothing would make her happier than seeing the look on their faces if Dick was right.

Chapter Thirteen
Life Goes On

Mark dropped Asia off at her house. As soon as she walked in the door of the place she had called home, it felt cold and uninviting. She didn't know how much longer she could stay there. With Howard gone, the way he was gone, and the place desecrated by thieves, there was no sense of home in this place anymore.

She poured herself into her work. Her job became her obsession now. She had spent the last several months representing the parents of a sixteen-year-old girl who had taken a summer job at one of the local upscale hotels. It was only part-time, but she enjoyed her job as part of the hotel's "hostess staff", especially knowing that with college in her future, she would not have to do this kind of work for a living. Also, the money gave her a greater sense of independence, not having to rely on her weekly allowance.

It was one afternoon at the hotel that she met a man named Ray Wilson. He had been staying at the hotel for a couple of days using one of the conference rooms to talk to teens and college students about his organization that worked to provide energy efficient housing to low-income families at no cost. His company, GREEN HOME,

DREAM HOME, would come in and rehab an old existing house using free labor from local students and leave behind an affordable green home when they were done. Their motto was "Help a family; save a planet." Unlike Habitat for Humanity, Ray's company dealt strictly with existing homes and only used local students to do the work.

Erin Allen's parents, Steve and Marsha, were surprised and proud when their daughter gave up her cushy job and the quest for more money to buy· the next new gadget in favor of the hard work helping those less fortunate than her.

They were even more surprised when after less than three weeks on the job, Erin abruptly quit going to work and spent her days locked in her room. It was only after crying for days and the constant coaching from her mother that she told of a sexual assault by Wilson that had taken place at one of the rehab houses. No one had witnessed the attack and Erin had washed away any forensic evidence. The police were not notified until her parents contacted them more than two weeks later.

Ray Wilson was a hero to the people he had helped, and they were willing to tell anyone who asked what a model citizen he was. His student volunteers would back them up. Erin, on the other hand, had trouble with delinquency at school and had several run-ins with the police since getting her driver's license. As a result, the prosecutors refused to bring criminal charges based on the lack of evidence and the credibility of the accused and the accuser. That left only a civil case for Asia to pursue and that wasn't going well either; but she was busy, and that was a good thing.

Mark was having a difficult time getting used to his new life too. In a matter of days, everything about who he thought he was had been turned upside side down.

He listened to his old radio spot, and it saddened him to hear the computer-generated formula smooth jazz music replacing the old school R&B show he had worked so hard to perfect. He wondered how many listeners had been lost, and how the countless letters and calls from his loyal fan base were being handled.

What else was missing during this upheaval was his social life. Prior to all of this, he had an active dating life, friends, and his SAA meetings to occupy his free time. Now, he had to make up things to do every day. One of which was to take the guns out of their locked hole in the safe room and take target practice in the woods next to the house. He would set up some cans and bottles on a fallen tree branch and fire away. It was fun, but he was a terrible shot. He did get fairly good with the handgun after a while, although the automatic made missing less of a problem and it was much more fun. With the automatic, he could just spray everything and watch the bottles and cans shatter and fly.

He also explored the woods surrounding his home and discovered his nearest neighbor was nearly six miles away. He chopped wood for the fireplace and dealt with the weeds that threatened to overtake the house if left unchecked. He found that he liked being outdoors, especially the fresh air in the morning. Whether working outdoors or hiking in the woods, there was always something to do rather than sit in the house and watch daytime television, but at the end of the day, the loneliness would set in.

Dick Price settled into his well-worn Barcalounger and turned on the television. He really didn't watch or listen to it. For Dick, it was mostly ambient noise.

It had been eight years now since his wife Ellen had passed, and the noise from the television helped him not to concentrate on his loss. The few shows he did take the time to watch were the quiz shows. He was good at them. Not as good as Ellen, but good.

He had earned a college degree at the insistence of his parents, and what he had learned about law enforcement came from being an investigator for the Army's Criminal Investigation Division (CID). That's where he first realized that he had an uncanny knack for recalling little known facts and information that he either heard or read over the years. It made him competitive at games and a good detective.

His small apartment was kept spotless, orderly, and well maintained. This was a sort of a tribute to Ellen, who spent an inordinate amount of time picking up after, cleaning up after, and admonishing her husband about his lack of tidiness.

"I'd hate to see this place after I'm gone," she would say, half-jokingly. Not knowing that their time together wound be so suddenly and violently brought to an end. A random purse snatching that had ended in murder.

No clues, no suspects; an eight-year-old cold case that no one was investigating. Dick had tried to look into it on his own, but at the time, his grief would not let him see or think clearly.

Johan Stannis was enjoying Silver City. This was his first time in the United States, and it was a welcome departure from Vietnam. Johan had always been big, even from birth, when he weighed in at a whopping eleven pounds. His mother was head housekeeper and cook for Raul's family.

In grade school, he stood five foot five. The muscle came later after he realized what an advantage his physical appearance gave him among his friends and especially his enemies. He had no training in the martial arts or conventional hand to hand combat. What he had was brute strength. He trained himself in the use of weapons, handguns in particular. He was a crack shot.

Raul's mother had noticed his size and strength early on and had told him as a child that she was entrusting him with a great responsibility; the safety and wellbeing of her son. Madame Hernandez, as she was reverently called now, was far from a nod to her former occupation. She had lost all vestige of a Madam. The profession that had originally brought her to Vietnam.

Johan grew up at Raul's side, making sure the boy was always accorded the respect due a prince. As a result, he and his mother were given privileges second only to the First Family.

Johan spent his time in Silver City enjoying the sights, especially the restaurants and nightclubs. He was a big hit in the clubs, where his size and physique attracted women like a magnet. His agility on the dance floor, a natural talent, just added to his popularity.

Johan was enjoying it here. He was staying at one of the finest hotels with a limousine at his disposal and unlimited cash. Since Raul kept such a low profile, most people assumed Johan was rich of his own accord. That was fine with Raul. He let Johan live out his fantasy. He spent his time in the city at his computer or on his phone overseeing the various companies he managed. He only met with Fred and Amir in person, and then only in out of the way surroundings, where they were less likely to be seen or remembered by anyone.

It was these meetings that raised Raul's frustration with the two. They seemed incapable of handling the situation, grasping at any long shot to locate the attorney with little in the way of results.

Raul felt that the wife was the key. He was unaware that the girl he had sold to Howard those many years ago was the woman he now felt could undermine his entire operation. He had some local contacts that would be better suited to finding out where the police were at in investigating the death of the girl and finding the attorney. He needed Fred to concentrate on the wife. His patience was running thin and his time in the city was running out; neither one was disappearing faster than his tolerance of their incompetence.

Chapter Fourteen
Tatiana

Fred and Amir were growing both desperate and scared. Each time they met with Raul, he seemed to grow angrier and more threatening. They instinctively knew the consequences of failure. Raul was not the kind of man to leave himself open to being exposed as a criminal; a criminal of the worst sort, a child sex trafficker. He had directed them to use his contacts to deal with Howard. Instead, in a panic, they had used local "talent" and now Howard was dead without disclosing anything. That should have been the end of it, except Fred remembered Howard's obsession with film. He had witnessed Howard with his movie camera capturing their trips to Raul's compound and providing copies to those who desired to replay their memories.

Back then, nobody gave any thought to the future, when the sexual exploitation of children would be front and center in the public's eye. Back then no one cared if you looked at any kind of pornography in the privacy of your home, and nobody had any idea that for the right price you could experience your deepest, darkest, desires without being labeled a criminal. No one was concerned with protecting the innocence of children. It wasn't on anybody's radar. They had never seen it coming until the rash of new laws and prosecutions began. People were going to jail for downloading and sharing pictures that just a few decades ago were considered adult entertainment.

There was outrage and condemnation now. Those sent to prison were called "short eyes" and more often than not suffered the same fate as the children they abused, or worse. Yet none of this seemed to matter to those who felt they were wealthier, more powerful, and smarter than the average sex offender at his computer. Their computers were clean. No cyber trail or electronic evidence of their crimes. Things were done in person in complete privacy, with a professional organization dedicated to protecting their identities.

The only weak link was from within, from people like Howard, who either through fear of incarceration or crises of conscience could place them all in jeopardy.

No one suspected that Howard was a weak link. After all, he had gone to prison without giving up any names of his associates. He had always been a stand-up guy. It was only when he felt guilty and threatened after the girl's death, that he let Fred know that if anything were to happen to him, he had hidden damaging information in an attempt to serve as a life insurance policy.

It was the unfortunate death of the girl that led to all of this.

That girl, Tatiana was her given name; Valentina was what she was called when she arrived at one of Raul's private "homes" or "dormitories" had been a happy child.

The only child of loving parents. The family was not wealthy but managed to make a modest living. Her father was a baker and her mother was a seamstress. They managed enough money to give their daughter private violin lessons from one of the local teachers. The girl had shown a talent for the instrument at an early age.

At the age of eight, she could be trusted to walk the two blocks from her house to her teacher's studio. She had made the short trip many times without incident. The neighborhood was middle class and safe by Russian standards.

Everyone knew little Tatiana and her little violin case. A pretty girl with blond curls, blue eyes, and an infectious laugh.

There was a state of shock and disbelief when, on her way to one of her lessons, little Tatiana simply disappeared. No one saw or heard anything. She just vanished, her violin case left on the street as if abandoned by its owner. The whole town and the neighboring towns joined in the search. The local police, ill-equipped to handle anything close to this, brought in government investigators to lead the search effort. After months of searching the surrounding area and canvasing the neighborhood residents for any clues, the disappearance of Tatiana Ivanov became a cold case.

Tatiana had arrived in Silver City in an unmarked van along with about ten or so other girls and boys of various origins and ages. They were housed in a converted warehouse in the business district of the city. The children were watched over day and night by several men and women whose sole purpose was to keep them fed and quiet. Tatiana had been in several cities in the last few months, none of which she ever saw. The children never left the "dormitory" except to "work". No one ever came to visit. They were simply escorted out at night to wherever they were requested and escorted back when their work was done.

Over the years, Tatiana had become numb to the experience. In the beginning, she had been known as a crier, always calling for her mother or father and refusing to answer to her new name. She was ·one of the few children who were not orphaned, abandoned, or sold to traffickers. Most of the others had little or no knowledge of family. Tatiana had been grabbed from the street because she was the right age and had natural blond curls, blue eyes, and a pretty face. A major request of many of Raul's clients.

Tatiana had always been frail, another thing many of the men found appealing, though it made her susceptible to bruising, illness, and broken bones over the years. She was now near the end of her usefulness, and her age and fragility both meant that Silver City could probably be the end of her time with Raul.

She knew this, which was why she kept silent when she began to feel sick and hurt again. She had witnessed firsthand the fate of girls and boys who were no longer physically able to meet the expectations of clients. It was why she made no friends of the many children she had seen come and go. The ones that left were hauled from their beds in the middle of the night and never seen or spoken of again. Mostly they were sick, hurt, or older, and now Tatiana was all three.

The night of her death, Tatiana fell deathly ill. The men were getting impatient with her and becoming more and more aggressive in their efforts to get her to respond. She did her best, but she just couldn't. She did not know Howard, but she could see from his face that he desperately wanted this to stop. She pleaded with her eyes for anyone to recognize that she was not being uncooperative. But people had paid their money and they wanted what they paid for.

The men began to slap and hit her with greater and greater intensity. Raul would have stopped it. He would not have stood for it. He would have taken control of the situation and she would have survived, at least for the evening. But Raul was not there. It was not until everyone noticed that she was gone that they came to their senses. It was like they all had been in some collective state of frenzy, pulling and thrusting at her, each trying to get his share, led by a man she would never know as Fred Randolph, a respected career U.S. diplomat.

When Fred realized what had happened, his immediate concern was not for the girl. His thoughts were of Raul. He was the one who had arranged for the girl to come to Silver City and therefore, he would be the one Raul would hold responsible, along with Amir, for the loss of his "property". They were on the hook to clean up this mess quickly and quietly. The consequences of the loss would be dealt with later.

Had Fred been thinking properly, he would have asked for Raul's help in disposing of the body where it would never have been found. But in a moment of panic, the decision was made to dump her far away from any place connected to any of the participants. Hopefully, she would be designated as a "Jane Doe", probably a runaway, working the streets as a prostitute who happened to be picked up by the wrong "John".

No one thought of the fact she would be identified as someone not from the U.S. based on her dental work and lack of U.S. required vaccinations. The police were now actively involved, suspecting a child trafficking ring was in the city.

Chapter Fifteen
Bad News?

It was late afternoon when Mark went into town to pick up his local newspaper. There was no delivery where he lived, and he enjoyed the ride into town. As usual, he read the headlines before taking the paper home to read at it at his leisure. The shock made him dizzy and for a second he lost his balance. Just below the fold was the story of two men found shot to death, execution style, near the riverfront. One was a U.S. diplomat, the other a distant relative of the royal family of Dubai.

There were no clues; no suspects, no anything, except for the fact that the men had been shot in the back ·with a large caliber weapon and the bodies had been moved from the original site of the murders. No attempt had been made to hide their identities. The prevailing suspicion was that the murders were meant to send a message; no clue as to who the message was meant for.

Mark didn't know what to feel. Was he now in the clear or, more likely, was he now in greater danger? His next thought was to call Asia. He made the call right there at the newsstand rather than trust the spotty cell service at his home.

Chapter Sixteen
Monk

When Mark joined SAA, he saw many people come and go on a regular basis. Some quit, some went to jail, and some died. Most of them he never really got to know, except one.

Monk was a dark skinned black man, about five foot nine inches tall and muscular. He looked mean and angry most of the time, except when he shared his story. He then took on the air of a well-educated, sophisticated man. He belonged to both SAA and NA, (Narcotics Addicts Anonymous). He had been incarcerated in Silver City's notorious jail on several occasions and had the scars to prove it.

Mark thought that this was a man that you knew wasn't worried about being abused in prison. If any abusing was to be done, he was going to be the one doing it.

Monk would come to meetings regularly for about three or four months then disappear for five or six, so it was a surprise when one night Monk asked Mark to be his sponsor. They talked regularly on the phone, even when Monk wasn't coming to meetings. Since his last jail stint, Monk had somehow managed to get a job as the facilities manager at a mid-sized low income apartment complex in the inner city. He was married to an Irish woman he met in drug rehab. Over the months, he and Mark had become close and shared some of their most closely guarded secrets. He was a man Mark thought he could truly trust and vice versa. After calling Asia, Mark made his next call to Monk.

"Got a minute?"

"Sure, what's up?"

Mark spun out the whole story, every detail. There was silence on the other end. Finally, Monk said: "Wow. If I didn't know you, I'd swear you had one of those relapses where an addict makes up shit to cover his acting out."

"This is real."

"Why the hell tell me?"

"Because if anything happens to me or the lady I told you about, there will be somebody who knows why."

"And just what am I supposed to do with that?"

"Maybe go to the police?"

"Now you're hallucinating. What makes you think with my record the police would believe anything I say? Hell, they would probably think I did it."

"At least someone would know that it wasn't an accident or suicide."

"Small comfort. What are you doing to protect yourself and your lady?"

"She's not my lady."

"So you say."

"I've moved to the outskirts of the city, way out in the middle of nowhere. I quit my job and I have weapons stashed away."

"Sounds like a good start."

If nothing else, Mark felt better that someone other than he and Asia knew what was going on. He had no doubt that when it came down to it, Monk would find a way to do the right thing.

Chapter Seventeen
Choices and Questions

Persons unknown weren't the only ones looking for Mark. The minute Dick Price saw the morning news, he knew he'd been right from the beginning.

Mrs. Peabody's description of the men outside Mark's apartment were obviously the two men found dead by the river. His instincts told him that this lawyer was not a cold blooded killer. Someone or some people wanted to find this guy and they were disappointed with the results thus far.

Bill Paterson was the lead detective assigned to the murders. So far he had made no connection between the dead girl and these new murders, and probably never would. Bill and his partner Buzz were by the book guys. Thinking outside the box was not their strong suit.

Dick, on the other hand, had always gone with his gut and being assigned to the burglary unit wasn't going to get in his way. He was on to something and he was not about to let it go. The thing that puzzled him most was the woman, the wife. What part, if any, did she play in this? Was she just an innocent person caught up in something she knew nothing about, or was she the key to the whole thing?

Johan was on to something too. This lawyer knew something; that much Fred had uncovered. Now the guy had disappeared. Nobody knew where he was.

He was running, not going to the police, but running. Whatever information he had, he wanted to keep it to himself.

Mark was in contact with Asia daily now, trying to figure out their next move. The fact that Fred and Amir had been murdered made them think twice about going to the police. Asia assured Mark that Raul would not stop simply because the police were involved. She was afraid that he was already in the city. If he was, she and Mark were not safe. Raul was cleaning house. Going to the police was no guarantee of safety.

Mark pleaded with her to move in with him temporarily. He had enough room, and she would be safer than in her house. She declined, but said she would think about it. Days went by and they were no closer to figuring out what to do than they were than when they first made the discovery. The good news was they believed Asia was still under the police radar.

Dick was coming up empty trying to locate Mark. Had he really left the city, maybe even the country? Leaving the country was unlikely; he wasn't a rich man, unless there was money or a check in that envelope. He could, however, have left the city or even the state. He did have a duffel bag with him when he and Artest interviewed him at the station. He personally now kept in contact with Bill and Buzz, who still couldn't figure out why Price was so interested in their cases. Dick's reputation for having a nose for things led them not to protest too much.

Johan was also having trouble with the whereabouts of Mark. He was also thinking about the envelope. Was it a check? A letter telling him where to find something important? What? Howard was a cautious man. He stayed within his trusted group of friends. If he left a personal letter, or whatever, to someone, then that person was no stranger.

Johan had another piece of the puzzle that Dick did not. He had checked out Howard's house to see who came and went and he had recognized Asia. It had been years, but he was sure it was the same girl from Vietnam.

Chapter Eighteen
No Hiding Place

Mark found that loneliness was the hardest part of living by himself. On occasion, he would travel into the city and have a nice meal or take in a show. It took the edge off and he stayed away from the more popular places. That house had now begun to drive him claustrophobic.

It was on one of those visits to town, when leaving a tucked away restaurant, that Mark got a shock. It was Joe Stanton!

"Mark, is that you?"

"Joe?"

"Yeah, it's me. I didn't know you ate here."

"Well, I don't really, just stepped in for a bite and pick up a newspaper."

"You got a minute? Come back in, have a drink. Tell me what you've been up to."

"Love to Joe, but I've got to run, just stopped by to grab a bite to eat."

"You sure? The boys at the station would love to hear how you're doing."

"Tell them I'm doing fine. Really miss the guys."

"Well, are you working? Where at? Did you get that personal stuff straightened out?"

"No, not yet. Just taking a break for a while."

"Wow, I didn't know you had that kind of coin. Must be nice."

"Yeah, I had a little saved up."

Mark could not wait to get away, but Joe was in no hurry. "So where are you staying?"

"I've been moving around a lot. Haven't found a place I like yet."

"Well, let's plan lunch. You like this place, I like this place. What's a good day?"

"I've got your number, I'll give you a call."

"Don't forget. I'll tell the fellas I ran into you."

"Yeah, please do that."

They shook hands and Mark went off in a different direction from his car. Something struck Joe as odd. Mark didn't seem quite himself. He knew they had not parted under the best of circumstances but he felt something else just wasn't right. It wasn't until later on, as he was leaving work, that he remembered that the detectives had given him their cards and asked him to call if he ever heard from Mark.

Johan felt his best chance of finding this lawyer was Asia. She had to know something. He spent his time ·parked a little way up the street from her house and followed her every time she left. It was boring, but after she turned out her lights, which was generally pretty early, he was free to enjoy the rest of his evening.

Monk wasn't too worried about Mark. He felt good that he had found a safe place to stay. Mark's "lady friend" was another story. He took up spending evenings he wasn't at a meeting parked down the street from her house, only leaving after her lights went out.

Joe Stanton did what he was asked to do and notified Price that he had seen and talked to Mark.

Artest thought it didn't make sense, what Price asked her to do. Mark wasn't about to go near that restaurant again after what happened with the station manager. Dick explained his thinking—it wasn't about the restaurant; it was about the newspaper. People are creatures of habit and if Mark never planned to go to that restaurant again, he might still get his newspaper nearby. Her job was to keep an eye on the local newsstand within walking distance of the restaurant. She didn't see this as anything other than a long shot, but he was Dick Price and she trusted his instincts.

Asia called Mark in a panic. He could barely understand her due to the intermittent cell service. He could make out that she had noticed two cars that were not the usual parked on her street, one down and the other up from her house. They just sat there and never moved. She felt she was being watched.

Mark told her that he would come and pick her up. She didn't need to pack, they had money for whatever she would need. On his way to get her, thinking there was no real rush, he decided to pick up his newspaper on the way.

It was not all that surprising to Artest that Dick's "creature of habit" theory proved true. With only a day of surveillance, Mark Brooks showed up just two blocks from the restaurant. He bought his paper and returned to his car. She followed.

Johan watched as a car pulled up to the Goldstein home. The man in the car fit the description that he got from Fred. Mrs. Goldstein came out and the two drove off. He thought the car that began following them might be a police escort, but he wasn't sure. He followed the two cars. Monk watched as Mark drove away and saw the two cars follow him. He joined in the pursuit.

Chapter Nineteen
End Game

They headed toward the outskirts of the city like a small caravan. For a while it appeared as if they were going to no particular destination. It came as a surprise to everyone when Mark turned down a long desolate road. You could barely see the lone house in the clearing. The caravan kept going past the turn off. Artest called Price and told him that she had located Mark Brooks and was on her way back to pick him up.

Johan watched her turn around and assumed that her escort duties were over. He decided that his best option was to come back after dark and take care of both Mark and Asia. This was perfect; out here, out of sight or earshot of anybody. There was no need for any elaborate plan. He called Raul and let him know that everything would be taken care of that evening and continued to drive away.

Monk turned around and headed back to the city. Artest was behind him now, so he slowed down to let her pass. She couldn't help but wonder what the black guy was doing out here where it seemed that Mark was the only resident; could be a friend, or just someone lost. Monk pulled over to the side of the road and pretended to be on his cell phone to help create the illusion.

After the SAA meeting, which ran over as they sometimes did, Monk decided to drive out to Mark's place and tell him what he had witnessed, despite the hour. He would have called but Mark had mentioned the spotty cell service. When he arrived, there was already a car parked at the top of the road leading to the house. Monk parked his car and headed down the road on foot, thinking that this was not a good sign. Why would someone park this far from the house? His sense was that something was way wrong. Mark had said there were people looking to harm him.

Johan had arrived just seconds before Monk and casually walked toward the house. It was pitch black and there didn't appear to be any lights on. If they were asleep, his job had just gotten a lot easier.

Mark was completely focused on Asia after he picked her up. Seeing how upset and scared she was made him feel the same. She had not said a word on the trip to the house. He was so preoccupied with Asia that he never looked in his rearview mirror.

Once they were at the house, he suggested that they spend the night in the bunker. She did not protest. Once down there, they both felt a little safer. Mark draped off a section for Asia—the part with the bed, shower, and toilet. He set up a cot for himself and retrieved one of the handguns from the hole, loaded it, and set it down on the floor next to the cot.

Feeling restless, Mark noticed and old record player in the corner of the room next to a stack of vinyl albums. Looking through them, he found one he liked. It was Aretha Franklin's recording of Curtis Mayfield's "Sparkle".

Just the kind of music he would play when he had his DJ spot. When Asia heard the music, she shouted from the shower, "Oh, I love that album, turn it up!"

Mark cranked up the volume. It was good to see her finally starting to relax.

Johan began searching for his best entry point. He circled the house, thinking he would catch them in bed sleeping. He was just about to break in the back door when he heard music. He noticed the small door under the house and put his ear to it to be sure. Johan stepped back and fired twice with his made to order "hand cannon". The 1950's-era wooden doors were no match for the powerful weapon. Johan reached down and opened the exposed hole in the door.

The shots and Asia's scream made Mark fumble to reach the gun by the cot. By the time he reached it Johan was already pointing his gun at Mark. At that moment there was a loud shout from outside. "Hey Mark!"

For a spilt second, Johan, startled, turned his head to see who was behind him. In that split second Mark fired two shots and Johan fell dead inside the bunker.

Dick Price wasn't buying the "lost guy on the lonely road". His gut told him this guy was involved. After their shift, he and Artest drove out to Mark's house. It was late, but Dick wanted answers, especially if Mrs. Goldstein was there too. They arrived just in time to hear gunfire. Both loudly announced themselves, drew their weapons, and entered the bunker. Johan lay dead on the floor. Mark and Asia were standing there holding each other and the mysterious black man was sitting on the cot.

Once they composed themselves, they told the detectives their story and showed them the videos. Something they had not noticed before were glimpses of the dead man on the tapes. They made no mention of the duffel bag. Dick told Artest to radio headquarters and put a BOLO (be on the lookout) for Raul not knowing that Raul, thinking that Johan had things under control, had left for Vietnam on his private jet hours ago. No matter, the Vietnamese police and Interpol would soon have copies of the tapes and would take it from there.

When Bill and Buzz arrived on the scene early in the morning, they were more than embarrassed that Dick and Artest had solved the Howard Goldstein "suicide", the murders of Tatianna, Fred, and Amir, and exposed an international child sex trafficking ring—all in one night. They gave no congratulations or handshakes.

Several days later, about a dozen or more children were found abandoned on the city streets. Raul's accomplices had shut down the "dormitory" and fled the city.

Later that month, Dick Price was promoted to chief of detectives. He immediately reopened the cold case murder of Ellen Price.

Artest was promoted to Detective Sergeant and patrolman James Jones became a newly promoted detective.

Mark and Monk spent several nights on the town and became much more than Sponsor and Sponsee. They became friends, best friends.

Mark and Asia went out on their official first date. It went well, very well.

In the following months, several high-ranking politicians, corporate executives, high profile entertainers, prominent sports figures and clergyman were arrested and charged based on their appearance on Howard's tapes.

Just how Howard Goldstein came in possession of a duffel bag filled with money and bonds remains a mystery.

The End